The Little Pine Tree's Christmas Dream

Clarence Thomson

Illustrated by Denise Dian Laughlin

 PAULIST PRESS

New York/Mahwah, New Jersey

Library of Congress Cataloging-in-Publication Data

Thomson, Clarence, 1935-
    The Little Pine Tree's Christmas dream/by Clarence Thomson; illustrated by Denise Dian Laughlin.
        p.   cm.
    Summary: Afraid that he will never be a Christmas tree, Little Pine Tree sheds tears that freeze into icicles and lead a family to choose him.
    ISBN 0-8091-6614-3 (paper)
    [1. Christmas trees—Fiction. 2. Christmas—Fiction.] I. Laughlin, Denise Dian, ill. II. Title.
PZ7.T37385Li   1993
[E]—dc20   93-5301
                                                                         CIP
                                                                          AC

Published by Paulist Press
997 Macarthur Blvd.
Mahwah, N.J. 07430

Printed and bound in the United States of America

or my son

Steve

who heard it first

Once upon a time there was a Little Pine Tree with a dream. His dream was to be a beautiful Christmas tree, surrounded by a happy family, presents, music and the Christ Child.

*B*ut tonight the dream seemed far away. He was sitting in a vacant lot, watching all the people shopping for Christmas trees and not one of them even seemed interested in him.

*T*hey all looked at bigger or straighter trees or, perhaps, they just didn't see him. He sighed and his needles drooped.

ust then a family came in. Their little boy came running over with his older sister who was trying to slow him down. The little boy shouted at his parents, "This is the one I want, it's just right for us!"

*H*is parents and older sister just looked, nodded and said, "Oh, yes, it is a nice tree, but we need to look over the others and see if there are any we like better."

*O*ff they went, with the little boy fussing and looking back over his shoulder.

The Little Pine Tree was crushed. He'd gotten his hopes up so high when the boy ran over to him. He had heard the little boy say so clearly, "This is the one I want." The tree's heart had leaped. He had been certain that this was his moment, his chance for his dream to come true.

But now he was alone. A shiver ran up and down his branches and several needles shook off. And then he began to cry. First, just a few tears and then more and more tears began to run down his needles.

And as they did, the cold December night froze his tears to the needles and the cold tears formed long icicles. He didn't care. It seemed as if he was never going to be a Christmas tree anyway.

The family with the little boy didn't find a tree that suited them. They had discussed and argued a bit, but could not decide on one. They started to leave the lot. Just then the little boy spotted the Little Pine Tree with all the icicles of tears off to one side.

The lighting was not very good in the parking lot, but the moon was oh, so bright! The Little Pine Tree's icicles gleamed in the moonlight.

*W*hen the little boy pointed to the tree, his mother sighed:

"Look at it now."

"It is exactly what we want," his dad exclaimed.

"Everybody will love it," his sister echoed.

*T*he little boy danced around the tree, saying: "It is the one I chose! We are going to get my favorite tree."

They loaded up the tree on top of their car and drove home with it.

When they decorated the Little Pine Tree for Christmas, they put little tinsel icicles all over its branches to remind them of how beautiful they were in the moonlight.

*T*he Little Pine Tree's dream had finally come true! He was the center of Christmas for the family. Presents surrounded him, he stood right next to the crib of the Infant Jesus, carols were sung, and everyone admired him.

Ever since that time, Christmas trees have had little tinsel icicles sprinkled all over them to remind us all of the Little Pine Tree whose dream had come true.